FROM *his* *Lips*

(53 LETTERS #1.5)

LEYLAH ATTAR

This novella contains SPOILERS.
It is meant to be read after the full length novel,
53 LETTERS FOR MY LOVER.

PITCH73 PUBLISHING

10 9 8 7 6 5 4 3 2 1

ISBN: 978-0-9937527-5-9 (pbk.)

Printed in the United States of America

PITCH73 PUBLISHING
TORONTO, CANADA

For the girls at Leylaholics Book Nook,
and all the readers, bloggers and amazing new friends—
there are no words for the support you have shown me.
This book would not have happened without you.

1. GROUND ZERO

I WAS IN A BLACK MOOD, AND THERE WAS NOTHING I COULD do about it except bury myself in more work. Tina skulked into the office, hugging the walls like she wanted to disappear into them.

"Here you go, Mr. Heathgate," she said.

I could almost hear her gulp as she left the documents on my desk, before scurrying back out. I was half-way through of a long column of figures when my phone rang.

"Why are you calling my cell, Sam? What do we have land lines for?"

"Sorry, Troy. It's Saturday. I didn't think you'd be at work. Is this a bad time?"

"Cut to the chase," I growled.

He launched into our latest project. I should have been listening. So much depended on it. But all I could think about was *her*. I had made an art of avoiding her for four years. Four long, miserable years that hung like a thundery, grey cloud over me. It was there when I opened my eyes in the morning, turning everything dull and foggy. Once in a while, I managed to escape, to jump-start the adrenaline and feel alive again. Biking treacherous paths in Bolivia;

ice-climbing the Rocky Mountains; giving in to the crazy thirst for a pair of golden arms and legs. But when morning came, I was back to grey. Ground Zero. Until yesterday—a truly drab, rainy day that had burst into a kaleidoscope of spectacular color the moment I'd stepped into Jayne's car.

And there she was. In the passenger seat.

Shayda Hijazi.

Damn her. Damn her golden, glowy skin and her liquid brown eyes. Damn the way she'd looked at me like I was the apocalypse, knocking on her door. Damn the way her voice quivered when she'd said hello. But most of all, damn her for having this friggin' hold over me.

I ran my fingers through my hair, wishing I could wipe yesterday clean, start over and head in the opposite direction so I was nowhere near Jayne and her stalled car. Seeing Shayda again was like getting a sniff of the drug you had sworn off, the one that could kill you, but still called to you, wanting to get in your blood and turn your insides out. I focused on Sam's voice, trying to clear my head as I stared out the window.

"Miss? MISS! May I help you?" I heard Tina's voice before the door to my office swung open.

And there she was again. Two days in a row. Shayda Hijazi. My deadly narcotic. My fix. My fixation. My opium. Except she was like a field of blazing poppies—soft, swaying petals that made me forget all about the poison seeds; standing before me in a prim and proper dress that made me want to slide my hands under the full skirt and rip her panties off.

"Sam, I'll call you back," I said before hanging up.

"I'm sorry, Mr. Heathgate, she just—"

"Thank you, Tina. That'll be all."

Tina hesitated, her eyes darting from me to Shayda, before seeing herself out and shutting the door behind her.

And then it was just me and Shayda. Well, technically, it was me, Shayda and the whole charged-up field that always zapped between us, like mini bolts of blue lightning. I stood motionless, speechless, afraid she'd take off, afraid she wouldn't.

"I got the umbrella," she said, after what seemed like an eternity of holding my breath.

"Good."

"Doesn't look like I'm going to need it today."

"No."

"Well. I just came by to say thanks," she said, shifting uneasily under my gaze.

It wasn't until she reached for the door that I moved.

No.

I'm not done looking at you.

I'm not done filling myself up on your face and your fingers and your feet and your soft, sexy voice.

"Don't go." I shut the door, bracing my arms on either side of her as she stood with her hand on the door knob, her back to me.

God. I'd missed her—the rose scent of her skin, the way her hair grew on her nape, the perfect, delectable ears that I could swallow whole in my mouth. It took steel-edged control to stop myself from grabbing her waist, from spinning her around and unleashing my pent-up passion on her lips, her breasts, her curvy-assed body. I wanted to slam her against the door and ravage her until she let out those little kitten moans that drove me wild.

"Can I get you some coffee?" I forced myself to step away. Another second and she'd feel my worked up cock pressing into her.

It worked. She turned and followed me to the mini-bar.

I poured her a cup and waited for her to take it, but she just stood there, staring at my fingers around the mug.

"Here." I placed it on the counter.

It killed me that she didn't want to risk touching me. It thrilled me too. Because it meant she wasn't immune to it. But mostly, it killed me.

"Cream? Sugar?" I knew exactly how she liked it. Tea. Coffee. Sex.

"Aren't you having any?" she asked.

She wanted me to have coffee with her.

In my mind we were fucking. Gloriously, furiously fucking.

I poured myself a cup and stared into the steaming brew of irony, hating myself, hating her. It was the only way I could keep myself from looking at her, because then she'd see it—my endless, boundless need for her.

"Troy?"

"Yes?" I took a peek because now she was the one hiding her face, averting her eyes.

"I don't want coffee." A tear rolled down her face.

A *fucking* tear.

"Don't, Shayda." It took every bit of restraint, not to clasp my hand over hers.

"I don't want coffee," she said. "Or cream. Or sugar."

"I know, baby. But it's all we got." *Because I get why you shut me out. Because the only way I can make this right is to take you away from everyone you love. Because no matter which scenario plays out, someone always gets hurt.*

"We've got today," she whispered.

"What are you saying, Shayda?" I held my breath.

"I'm saying, we have now. Here. Today."

"Quit fucking with me, Beetroot." There was a deadly warning in my voice. *I don't want today. I want all your todays.*

But the moment I said her pet name, I knew I was done. She was my Beetroot Butterfly. She might stop to rest on my shoulder, let me hold her for a while, my palms outstretched, let me marvel at her fragile, fleeting wings, but the slightest breeze and she'd be gone, taking with her all my colors.

Because she wasn't mine to love. Or to have, or to hold. She wore a shiny gold band around her finger, and it wasn't mine. She had worn it since the first time we'd met.

2. STILLNESS

....

I WOKE UP THAT DAY WITH A FOOT IN MY FACE. NO NAIL polish. Rough, hard, big and hairy. A man's foot.

Disappointing.

"Ryan." I pushed his dangling leg back on the bed. My voice was raspy from all the beer, and my head felt dull and heavy.

"What?" He stirred.

"I'm going for a run. You still in?" I got off the floor and stretched. I had carpet burn from where I'd crashed last night and the rosary around my neck had left round indents on the side of my arm.

"Are you kiddin' me?" he mumbled. "Go back to sleep and think happy thoughts of Matilda."

"Mmmmmmatilda." I smiled. The exchange student Ryan's girlfriend had hooked me up with.

"Dude, her body did *not* match her name." said Ryan.

"Dipshit." I smacked him in the back of his head. "Is that why you had Ellen set us up?"

6

"I could only hope. But you always luck out. Now get out of my face." He pulled the covers over his eyes.

I should be sleeping too, considering what time we got back. Thank god for Ellen. I'd been in no condition to drive myself home. I dusted the sand off my sweatshirt and put it on. Beach parties are fun. And gritty. And I was still smelling of smoke and whatever perfume Matilda had on. I thought about hitting the shower, but I was going to get sweaty anyways.

It was early enough that dew drops still clung to plump blades of grass. A cool, sunny June morning—perfect for a run. And that's exactly what I did. I ran. Not a nice, leisurely start to the day, but a full-on sprint, the incomparable rush of feeling the world whizz by in a blur of sound and light and color .

I'd been running since sixth grade. It was the only thing that had stopped the phone calls—the ones my parents used to get from school.

"We're a little concerned."

"He lacks focus."

"We asked the kids to hand in a report about their favorite book. Troy picked four. None of which he finished."

My curiosity was my downfall. I wanted to see everything, learn everything, taste everything. All at once. I snuck into classes not meant for me. Sex Ed when I should have been in Math. Splatter Painting when I should have been drawing apples in the Still Life class. I ate when I was hungry, instead of when I was supposed to. I talked in the library and whistled in class. I winked at girls and declared undying love for my fourth grade teacher. I was a disruptive, albeit charming, rule-breaker, and had to be dragged back to my desk countless times, by my ear.

It got better once I started channeling all my extra energy into running. My grades improved, I wasn't bouncing off the walls and kids weren't as intimidated by me. I leaned out, made the track team and kept running—even now, when I was in college. Why mess with a good thing, right?

I took a swig of water and spotted a pair of long-legged girls walking my way. Heck, I loved summer. Sweet things in tank tops and short shorts. They looked at me. One said something to the other and then they looked away. They stole another glance as they got closer, and giggled.

Women. So fucking irresistible. Coy, feisty, sporty, nerdy, glamour dolls, book worms, hot, cool. I was a slave to their charms. And it didn't hurt that they seemed to gravitate towards me.

"Morning, girls." I slowed down as they passed.

They smiled and batted their eyelashes. The blond elbowed the brunette and they laughed some more.

I turned around and watched them walk away.

Damn those short shorts.

I was still reverse-walking, my eyes on the sweet summer girls, when I collided into someone.

I say 'collide' because I didn't just bump into her. I sent her flying.

"Whoa! Are you all right? I didn't see you there."

She didn't reply. She was on her knees, trying to collect all the papers she'd dropped. They were quickly getting swept down the street. I intercepted one with my foot and ran the others down.

"Here you go." I knelt beside her and handed her the pile.

That's when I first saw her face.

At the time, I was completely clueless about just how significant that moment was, how it would derail both our lives, because at the time I was just an ordinary guy looking at an ordinary girl on a quiet, shaded street. That's how a lot of things start, don't they? Our most profound experiences, our greatest adventures. When we're just looking. Because if we knew that we were really at the beginning of miracles and plagues, and slayings and resurrections, we might retreat. But not knowing, I kept looking. And so did she.

Except she didn't just look *at* me, she looked *into* me. As if she saw a place there that she'd always wanted to go, and it stunned her that it actually existed.

I forgot the papers in my hand, forgot everything but the delicate starkness of her face. She wasn't cover-girl gorgeous. No. Her beauty came from some place deeper, some dark, hollow void that sucked up all of my scattered, restless energy. And for the first time I knew stillness. I was there, *all* there in that moment, not wanting to run off to the next one, or the one after that, or the one after that. Because that moment, that short, random suspension of me and her, was more loaded than anything I'd chased after.

She was wearing an ill-fitting yellow dress, buttoned up to the collar. Her hair was swept carelessly to the side. So much of it. Long, dark, curly. It glowed with red highlights where the sun touched it, like fiery pieces of stoked coal. She regarded me with eyes that were the shape of almonds; dark espresso eyes, flecked with cinnamon. She was singularly the most beautiful, exotic creature I'd ever seen.

Then she blinked and the moment was gone. Pretty soon she would be too.

"Shhh. Don't move," I said. "Not a muscle."

"Huh?" She turned a bright shade of red.

She had felt it too, and she was about to flit away.

"Don't move," I repeated. "There's a butterfly. On your shoulder."

Lame, but it was the only thing that came to mind.

"What color?" she asked.

"Red." *Like the glints in your hair, the flush on your cheeks.*

"Red?"

A lie.

I didn't care if she believed me. I just wanted her to stay. "It's the most beautiful thing I've seen," I said.

The truth.

"You know," I continued, grasping at straws to keep her there, "there's a Native American legend which says that if you want a wish to come true, you must capture a butterfly and whisper your wish to it. Since it makes no sound, it won't tell the wish to anyone but the Great Spirit. By making the wish and releasing the butterfly, your wish will be taken to the heavens and be granted."

"Are you...are you going to try and catch it?"

"Only if it wants to be caught."

Somewhere nearby, a rose bush was in full bloom. I could smell its sweet, heady fragrance in the air.

She made a short, jerky move, clamping down on the papers she was holding, as if to steady herself. Something glinted off her left hand. A ring. A plain golden band on her wedding finger.

Fuck.

All of the roving, tossing, turning energy found me again.

"It's gone," I said.

"What?"

"The butterfly." *The weird stillness I felt around you.* "Are you all right? You're not hurt, are you?"

"No," she replied.

But she looked unsure, like she wasn't sure exactly *what* had just happened.

That makes the two of us.

I smiled. "I'd say I'm sorry for running into you, but I'm not really."

Her guard was up now; her face back on. So that was the look she normally wore to keep the world at bay.

"Need some help?" I offered her a hand.

"I'm fine." She kept her head down.

Her right knee was scratched, but she was too busy clutching the papers like a shield to keep me away. It didn't seem right to just leave her there, in the middle of the street, but that's exactly what I did. Because I wanted to stay, and you don't mess with another man's woman.

I was tempted to turn around and make sure she was okay. Maybe I just wanted one final glance. She looked too young to be married.

Keep running, Troy. Keep running.

I had three more rounds to go, but I headed back to Ryan's. I felt like I had just been run over by a truck.

Ryan was sprawled out in the living room, watching TV and balancing a bowl of cereal on his lap.

"Hey," he said without turning around.

I peeled off my sweatshirt and downed the rest of my water. My throat still felt parched.

The doorbell rang.

"Dad! Are you expecting someone?" asked Ryan.

Bob came into the kitchen, finishing off his coffee.

"Would you mind getting that, Troy?" he said.

I opened the door and did a double take.

Yellow dress, curly hair, crooked pile of papers.

Her.

Standing upright, she was curvier than I thought. Not quite as tall. But she turned just as red when she saw my bare chested form.

Hell. I was ready to buy whatever she was selling. Cookies. Time share. Encyclopedia Fucking Britannica.

"Ryan?" she said, peering at me through the screen.

"I'm Ryan." His head popped up beside me. "He's Troy. Who are you?"

"Coming through, coming through," said Bob. "Oh hey, Shayda." He let her in. "Boys, this is my assistant. Be nice." He said something to her before leaving, but I wasn't listening.

I smelled roses as she walked past me and headed for Bob's home office.

"Holy crap. My dad's assistant? She's smokin'!" said Ryan, when she was out of earshot.

"Lay off, man. She's married."

We shut up as Ryan's sister walked into the hallway.

"You want breakfast?" she asked, rubbing her eyes sleepily.

"Since when, Jayne?" shot Ryan. "Should you even be up? It's not noon yet, is it?"

She was sixteen or seventeen, and her schoolgirl crush on me embarrassed Ryan, although he didn't say. He knew I would never make the moves on his kid sister. That's just part of the bro code.

"Shut up, smartass." Jayne flipped him the finger and gave me a honey-sweet smile. "You sure I can't get you anything?"

"Jayne, I'll look after breakfast," said her mother. "You go change."

Elizabeth Worthing was not impressed with her daughter's flimsy pajama shorts. Jayne made a face, but she went off to do her bidding.

"Morning, boys." Mrs. Worthing gave Ryan and me a peck on the cheek. "Have fun last night?"

Ryan groaned, nursing his head.

"How about you?" she turned to me. "You need an Advil too?"

I shook my head. My cotton-balled hangover had been knocked right out of me.

"God, you reek," she said, as I reached over and grabbed an apple. "Off to the shower, young man. You're not getting any pancakes until you've freshened up."

"Pancakes? Yummm." I took a big bite of the apple. "Thank you, Mrs. Worthing."

"Call me Lizzie," she said.

"Since when?" asked Ryan. First his sister and now his mum. "All my friends call you Mrs. Worthing."

"Lizzie, Mrs. Worthing. What difference does it make?" I heard her say as I headed for the bathroom.

"Hey, Jayne." Shayda's voice, coming from the study room. "Have you ever seen a red butterfly?"

Without the distraction of her unsettling presence, I could focus on other things. She had an accent—barely detectable, like she had practiced the words many times to iron it out, but it still lingered in the folds. It wasn't so much the way she said things, but the tone they took. High and low, up and down, a soft lilting like she was a bit unsure, so some words came out like question marks.

"A red butterfly?" replied Jayne. "Does that even exist?"

"Sure does." I peeked into the study.

They jumped liked they'd been caught in the act.

"I saw one just this morning," I said.

I had the funny feeling they'd been talking about me.

"Yeah, right." Jayne recovered first. "What's it called then?"

A full flush settled over Shayda's face when I looked at her.

"A Beetroot Butterfly." I smiled.

3. A BAR ACROSS THE STREET

MATILDA DIDN'T SPEAK MUCH ENGLISH, BUT WE communicated just fine.

"*Morgen,*" she said, her eyes fixed on my lips.

Kiss me.

Obviously.

I obliged.

"*Morgen.*" She laughed and said again.

"She wants to know if she'll see you tomorrow," explained Ellen.

"Morgen. Ja. Ja!" I nodded.

"Okay." Matilda smiled and got out of the car.

Jayne let herself in the front seat and stared sullenly after her. "She walks funny."

I laughed. Matilda walked sexy—with a seductive sway to her hips that got more pronounced when she knew she had eyes on her.

"I like her," I said to Ellen.

14

"I knew you'd get along," she replied. "She *really* likes you."

"So what else is new? Everybody likes Troy." Ryan slapped me in the back good-naturedly.

"But I like *you*," said Ellen, sidling up to him.

"Sheesh." Jayne rolled her eyes. "Now that we've cleared all that up, can we go? Mum said to be home by six."

With my parents out of town, Bob and Lizzie had taken me under their wing.

"Why don't you just stay here until they get back?" they said.

"Thanks, but I prefer my own space."

Truth is, I would have loved to stay. Lizzie was a mean cook, and Bob often took Ryan and me to work with him. We'd take pics of the properties he was listing and goof around at local hangouts until he was done.

But I couldn't stay. Because staying meant running into Shayda, and I didn't want to feel that intense awareness of her shoot through me. It made me feel alive and lousy at the same time, because I had no business thinking about her. So I accepted Bob and Lizzie's dinner invitation instead. She would be gone by then and I wouldn't have to wrestle with my misplaced reaction to her—look at her, don't look at her; talk to her, don't talk to her.

"Hey," Jayne rolled down her window and pointed to a Greek restaurant as we drove by a busy stretch of the road. "This is where Shayda works!"

"I thought she works for Dad," said Ryan.

"Yeah. In the day time. At night, she waitresses here."

"She has two jobs?" asked Ellen.

"Mmmm." Jayne nodded. "She's always working. She has to sponsor her family over from Tehran. I think her parents and brother are still there. She's only been here a year though."

"Mum said she had an arranged marriage," said Ryan.

"It wasn't arranged-*arranged*. Her aunt set them up when she moved to Toronto."

"You think her family got her married so they could all move here?"

"What do I look like? The six o'clock news?" Jayne swatted her brother.

"I'm just asking," said Ryan. "You two seem to have hit it off."

"How old is she anyways?" asked Ellen.

"Same as you. Twenty? Twenty-one? I'm not sure." Jayne shrugged. "She doesn't talk much about herself."

***

"ANY PLANS FOR CANADA DAY?" ASKED BOB.

"Not really. I'll probably just catch the fireworks at night," I replied. *With Matilda.*

"Can Ellen and I come over? You guys have such a fantastic view out on the lake," said Ryan.

"Sure. Consider yourself invited."

"Why don't you join us for lunch, Troy? Then you guys can head out together," suggested Lizzie.

"Thank you. You've just spoiled me with that delicious chicken. You know I'd never turn down your cooking." I smiled.

"I'll make something too," said Jayne.

"You?" Bob and Ryan looked like they'd just been smacked in the face.

"Yeah, me. You gotta a problem with that?"

"I'm glad you're taking an interest, Jayne." Lizzie hid a smile. "What's with the sudden domestication?"

"It's not sudden," Jayne protested. "I just didn't...you just don't know. None of you know." She sputtered indignantly.

"Well, I look forward to whatever it is you plan to serve us," said Bob.

"Sure. You have insurance," replied Ryan.

"Mom!" Jayne was not amused.

"I was thinking of inviting Shayda and her husband too," said Lizzie. "What do you think?"

"I think that would be fantastic," said Bob. "After everything they've been through, being around family would lift their spirits. Even if it's not their own."

"Why? What happened to them?" asked Jayne.

Bob and Lizzie exchanged a look.

"They've had a rough start," replied Bob.

A wild, unruly part of me crawled out from the ranks, wanting to know more, but I secured it, trapping the horned spider under an upside-down glass. I couldn't contain it too long though. The beast broke free on my way home.

I stopped at a bar and found a table by the window. So what if it happened to be directly across the street from the restaurant Jayne had pointed out, the place where Shayda worked?

One drink. Then I leave, I told myself.

But a man can make one drink last for a long time when he wants to. And so I sat there, ignoring the stares of women in clingy dresses, nursing a dry manhattan, as I watched the waitress across the street.

She was wearing the same yellow dress, with a green apron around her waist. Her hair was tied back and she occasionally tucked a loose strand behind her ears. The patio was full, the music loud. She seemed to be the only one serving the tables. In and out she darted, balancing trays of drinks and bread and entrees. She smiled when she was supposed to, talked when spoken to and brought the check at the end of the meal. It was as if she was there, and yet removed, like she had carefully stowed away the part of her that was her, and was moving around in a hollowed-out robotic assembly of hands and legs and eyes and face. It wasn't something you'd notice, unless you'd seen her, the *real* her, like I had for those few beats on the sidewalk. Because even momentarily, she had shone, so bright that I wondered what she'd be like if she were free and unrestrained.

I stayed until she turned the sign on the door to 'CLOSED' and the lights turned off inside. But she wasn't done. She came back out and watered the plants on the patio. She must have been dead tired, but this was the part she enjoyed. I could tell because she stroked the flowers gently, letting her fingers sing to them, perking up their tired, wilted forms after a hot, sunny day. Then she found a small table in the corner, away from the lights, and had her dinner.

Why was she sitting here alone? Why wasn't she hurrying home to have dinner with her husband?

Not your business, Troy. Not your business.

I watched as she tidied up, collected her things and walked to the bus stop. She was fumbling in her purse for change when the bus obscured her from my view. Then she was gone, an unknown commuter on a sleepy ride home.

I pulled out a few bills from my wallet and swallowed the last of my drink. I thought about calling Ryan and letting him know I was going to skip lunch tomorrow.

Hey, Ryan. Guess what? You know your father's assistant? Yeah, the one that's married. I just spent the last few hours stalking her. That's what I said. I sat across from her work and watched her. I wish I knew. She just gets to me, man. I feel like shit. I know. I'm gonna skip lunch tomorrow. I don't think I can sit across from her and her husband and make small talk. You get it, right?

I called Matilda instead.

4. EARTH AND SKY

PAST

MY ROOM FACED THE WATER. WHEN THE SUN CAME OUT, IT bounced off the lake and cast rippling strobes of light on the ceiling.

"So pretty." It fascinated Matilda. "Your home. So nice."

We'd spent half the night at a twenty-four hour burger joint, and the other half on the roof of my car, looking at the stars. It was nice, but now I was buzzing to go.

"I'm going for a run," I said.

She looked at me uncomprehendingly.

"A run. You know, exercise." I mimed.

"Ah. Ekzersize. I know best ekzersize."

She locked her heels around my waist. She had long, strong legs and eyes that reminded me of a jungle cat—pale green, but shot with gold. It was easy to lose myself in her wild embrace. This could be The Summer of Matilda. But I'd stopped last night and I was pulling away this morning.

"No like?" she asked.

I loved the way she said 'like'. Half-way between lick and like.

All hail The Summer of Girls With Sexy Accents.

"I like." I kissed her.

This was every guy's dream—a sweet, sexy, summer romp, at the end of which she'd head back home and I'd head back to college. I felt the rush of my response to her touch, her splayed-out hair, her big, wide pupils. But something didn't feel right. And that very word—'feel'—made me uncomfortable.

"I have to go for my run," I said.

"Okay. I go with."

She was sexy and sporty and cool.

I had to get my shit together.

This was *not* going to be The Summer of Regrets.

***

"Hey, Bob. It's Troy. Sorry, I'm not going to make it for lunch, but I'll be by later. No. Everything's fine. Yeah. See you soon. Thanks."

I'd called to make sure Ryan's family didn't wait for me, but they'd left the door open when I got there. There were no other cars in the driveway so I figured I'd timed it just right.

"Hello?" I called as I let myself in.

No answer.

I walked through the hallway, past the kitchen, and froze when I got to the living room.

Shayda was still here.

And she was looking out to the backyard, through the sliding door.

Why the fuck was she standing there alone? Where was her husband? Why wasn't she out there with everyone else?

I could see Ryan and Jayne goofing around with hoses in their hands. Then Bob and Lizzie got involved and soon the whole family was running and screaming and getting soaked.

All right. A water fight.

I could do a water fight. I could walk past Shayda, totally unaffected, and join in. This time it was different. This time I was prepared for whatever weird, walloping sensation might hit me, and I was ready to punch that sucker straight back to oblivion.

She didn't hear me walking up behind her. She was engrossed in the scene before her—all the laughing, hitting, yelling, squealing.

I was about to say something funny and silly and totally absurd. Then I caught her reflection in the glass.

You know those moments in childhood that completely floor you? Like the first time you see a dead bird or a dead squirrel and you realize that things die? You're momentarily seized with a longing to revert back to a time when you didn't know, a time of innocence and endless possibilities. That was the longing I saw in Shayda's eyes as she looked out the door—open, naked, unguarded longing.

I wanted to retrace my steps, wait at the traffic light instead of flooring it to make the amber; I wanted to sleep in a little longer, dally over the phone with my parents, stop at the gas station for chewing gum—anything to go back and add a few more seconds, a few more minutes, because then I would have missed it. The look on her face.

But it was too late. Our eyes met in the reflection as I stood behind her, and the look turned to shame and humiliation. The horror of being caught with your mask down. For a while, she just stood there, like a deer that knows it's been caught in the hunter's cross hairs. Then she bolted.

I seized her before she could escape, pinning her against the glass, my hand over hers, so I could anchor her, keep her from getting swept away.

Hey. It's okay.

She made a small, choking sound when I pulled her away from the sliding door. My arms went around her and her cheek found my chest. And just like that, something fell into place.

All of my wild, crazy exuberance fit perfectly in the quiet crevices of her dreams. It was as if all my life, I had been running towards this moment, this diamond sharp clarity of being and belonging, this strange, intriguing girl with her rose breath and her broken wings.

I didn't *want* to feel this. I wanted Matilda and wild, summer escapades and no strings. And *this* could never be *that*. *This* was so many strings that I felt like a puppet. She could contort me in a million different ways.

Run, Troy, run.

But I just stood there, holding her. Because I fucking *liked* having her in my arms.

It was as simple and as complicated as that.

∗∗∗

THE SUN HAD SET, BUT THE AIR WAS STILL HOT AND HUMID. Crowds of revelers had laid claim to their beach spots with picnic baskets and coolers and folding chairs.

"I'm so glad we don't have to hustle for space here," said Ellen. "Thanks for having us over."

"My pleasure." I replied. "We'd be there already if the traffic wasn't so bad."

"You think your car will be all right at the gas station?" asked Ryan.

"Greta said she'll look after it." I glanced back at Shayda. She was trailing along with Jayne.

It wasn't fair that she was here. I hadn't bargained for that.

We'd jumped apart when a loud splash brought us back to our to senses—Jayne pushing Ryan into the pool. She ran back to the house, squealing, when he threatened to come after her.

"Troy!" she said, when she saw me. "We've been expecting you."

I extracted myself from her ardent, puppy-love hug. "We?"

"I'm going too," she said. "And Shayda."

And so here I was, walking around like I was perfectly cool with it, when really I was in the ring with the twisted fuck called fate, slugging it out, one round at a time. This was not how I'd planned to catch the fireworks.

"So will Matilda join us later?" asked Ryan.

"Matilda?" Jayne caught up to us. "Matilda's not coming, is she?"

I laughed. When Jayne wanted something, she wanted something. And right now, she definitely did *not* want Matilda around.

"Matilda's host family had other plans for tonight. She's not going to make it."

The grin on Jayne's face. Like she'd just scored the last cookie in the cookie jar.

"It's not going to happen," I said.

"What's not going to happen?"

"Whatever you've got spinning in that delightfully stubborn head of yours."

"You think I'm delightful?" The grin grew wider.

She was impossible. And adorable. Like one of those wind up toys that just kept going and going.

Ryan rolled his eyes. "We better hurry or we won't make it to Troy's in time."

I glanced back and stopped. "Hey, where's Shayda?"

She was nowhere in sight. Behind us, the boardwalk was teeming with obscure figures, all jumbled up in a long trail of shadows.

"Does she know where we're heading?" I asked.

"No," said Jayne. "I didn't think to tell her."

"Shit." My eyes scanned the crowd. She could be anywhere by now.

"Why don't you guys go ahead?" I handed Ryan my keys. "No point in all of us missing the show."

"I'll go with you," said Jayne.

"You stick with Ryan and Ellen. I don't want risk losing you too."

"But—"

"Jayne." Ryan tugged her away firmly. "Let's go. You sure you don't need help, Troy?"

"I'll find her." I knew I would. Somehow. I'd always find her.

Yeah, dickhead. Find her, so you can let her go. The dirty bastard I was brawling with threw in a nasty jab.

Fuck off, fate. I'd forgotten about our sparring session.

Screw you, Troy.

We headed for our respective corners, temporarily suspending the match.

I parted my way through the surging mass of strangers, looking for Shayda. It wasn't too long before I spotted her. She was wearing a white dress in a sea of shorts and tees, getting jostled around in the crowd. She didn't seem to mind; it was as if she was used to being invisible, used to people having no regard for her.

My blood boiled as I made my way over and spun her around.

"Are you all right?" I asked.

"You found me." She blinked, as if she couldn't get around the fact that I'd come back for her.

"Of course." Had no-one told this girl that she mattered? That it was okay to push back instead of being pushed around?

I grabbed her hand and pulled her away from the crowd.

"Where are we going?" she asked.

I could have said, "My place," and headed back to meet up with the rest of the gang. But I didn't. Because I wasn't taking her there. I was going to test this girl's limits, push her until she pushed back, until she learned to stand up for herself and break free of that damn cocoon she'd built around herself.

Or maybe that was just a lie I told myself. Maybe I just wanted to spend some time with her.

Whatever. It didn't matter. Because by the end of the night, I had succeeded. I'd poked and prodded and goaded her until she lashed out. And god, she was magnificent when she was angry. All that fire and pain and bottled-up angst. I might have left a dent in her shell, a small chip where we collided, but in turn she cracked me wide open.

We might have had a chance then, to do it right. A small bud of 'perhaps' that could have bloomed and saved us from our ourselves. But she dropped a bomb on me that night, so big that I ran straight for the hills. Because I realized that it wasn't just about a faceless man I'd never met, it was about family and bonds and molds that had already been set.

"Goodbye, Shayda Hijazi," I said as the elevator doors closed on me.

"Goodbye, Troy Heathgate," she replied.

It was a few innocent hours that one night, The Summer I Met Shayda Hijazi.

5. ROSES

....

"I'd better see your sorry ass," said Jayne.

"I wouldn't miss it for the world," I replied. "I want to pass on my condolences in person. What's his name?"

"Matt. And you're just jealous because you lost out."

"Big time. And I know you're inviting me just so you can roast my heart on your big day."

"You don't have a heart."

"Ouch. Are you ever going to drop it?"

"That you dated every girl but me? Never." She laughed. "So shall I put you down for two?"

"Could you make that three?"

"Oh? I know it's been a while, but I had no idea you're a family man now."

"Not that kind of three."

"What other kind of three...?" Jayne trailed off. "Oh. *That* kind of three. Is that what's going on?"

"It is."

"I believe this is the first RSVP that's made me blush."

"You? Impossible," I teased.

"*You're* impossible."

"How's Ryan?"

"He's great. You know he and Ellen have two kids now, right? He'll be thrilled when I tell him you're moving back. It's been a while, huh?"

"I moved out here right after I finished college."

"Well, Toronto's waiting. We've missed you."

"I'll see you soon, Jayne. Give my best to Bob and Lizzie." I hung up and looked out at the New York skyline. I was going to miss this hustling, bustling centre—the noise, the smell, the constant, churning energy.

****

I smiled as I entered the banquet hall. Jayne Worthing was a little minx. And she hadn't changed one helluva bit.

"Where did you go, handsome?" Felicia pulled me aside. She was wearing a jewel-collared halter dress that showed off her sexy, tanned shoulders.

"I just checked in with the bride. I haven't seen her in years."

"Did you have a nice reunion?" asked Heather. She complemented Felicia perfectly in a black metallic sheath and dangling silver earrings.

"We did." I replied.

"I'll say." She wiped my mouth with her cocktail napkin and handed it to me.

Lipstick.

"You're a naughty boy," said Felicia.

"I think we should punish him tonight," Heather whispered in her ear.

"I think we should leave him out all together," she replied.

27

They turned their backs on me and walked off, hand in hand.

It was all part of the delicious games they played.

"Hey, Troy." I heard Bob calling me. "Troy!" He motioned me over. "I want you to meet Jayne's friend, Shayda. Also my brilliant protégée. She started off as my assistant and is now one of my top realtors."

She was sitting facing the other way, with her back to me. But she got up and greeted me with a smile.

Shayda Friggin' Hijazi.

I hoped I handled it just as well as she did—the shock of seeing each other again.

"Dad, they've already met," said Ryan. "Canada Day fireworks. Remember, Troy?

It was ironic that we were being officially introduced twelve years later. No-one had thought to to it then. Just as well, I thought. We were different people then. We are different people now.

"Yes," I said. "I remember." I shook hands with her.

Fuck. Same amped up crackling, rattling current, same jolt of electricity. Not the kind that sent me into overdrive, but the kind that zapped me into super-still awareness, where everything was heightened—sight, sound, touch, taste.

She looked brighter, shinier. Or perhaps it just felt that way—like putting a 'before' pic next to an 'after' pic. There were details I'd forgotten. Like the tiny scar that split her lower lip, and the way she averted her eyes if you looked at her too long. Her hair was up in a snug bun that would have looked severe, except that it highlighted the graceful curve where her ear met her jaw.

"They're here everyone!" said Lizzie, as Jayne and Matt made their entrance.

My hand settled on Shayda's back, nudging her forward so my frame wasn't blocking her view. It was an unconscious move, but I felt her entire body tense.

"There you are." Heather showed up by my side. "Did you forget about me?"

"Heather." A woman who didn't react to my touch like it was poison ivy. "Where's Felicia?"

"Right here, darling." Felicia gave me a kiss.

Apparently, they were done pouting.

We took our seats once the bride and groom were seated at the head table. Our place cards were right across from Shayda, Bob, Lizzie and Ryan. I had two of the most beautiful women in the room on either side of me, and I was struggling to keep my focus off Shayda. Every time my eyes rested on her, I had to willfully deflect them onto something else. It was like trudging through a marsh with lead weights on my feet.

What was she doing here alone? Where the hell was her husband? Did he even exist, or was he just a taunting specter, a shadow that had slipped on that golden ring, staked his claim, and then disappeared?

I took another swig of my drink.

"Slow down, babe." Heather ran her hand down my thigh.

"We're almost done with the speeches," said Felicia.

They thought my restlessness was catching up to me. I got up and headed to the bar for a refill.

When dessert was done and the music started, I let Felicia and Heather drag me to the dance floor. They were fun and free and exactly who I should be dancing with. Helicia.

"I wish you were flying back to New York with us," said Heather.

Felicia swayed provocatively against me. "We're going to miss you." Her hands slid under my jacket.

"Let's take it off." Heather slid it off my shoulders and nipped my ear. "So much yum."

"Let's keep it PG, girls," I said, leading them back to the table. "For now."

They sank into their seats, with no intentions of behaving.

"And why isn't the mother of the bride kicking up her heels?" I asked Lizzie. She was the only other person seated at the table.

"Food over frivolity," she replied, finishing the last of her dinner. "I'm a slow eater."

"With great timing." I held out my hand. "May I have the pleasure of this dance?"

"Why, yes. You may, sir." She smiled.

"It's so good to see you, Troy, " she said as we weaved between other couples on the dance floor. "How are Grace and Henry?"

"Mum and Dad are doing great. I'm glad you guys stay in touch."

"We're empty nesters. That's what we do—get together and reminisce about our kids."

"Please. You're too young to reminisce, Lizzie."

"And *you* are too old to keep cavorting with those..." She gestured towards Helicia.

"Who're you calling old? Thirty-three is prime time, woman!" I spun her into a series of dizzy turns.

She laughed and shrieked and held on to me when it was done.

"I think we're making Bob jealous," I said.

"I don't see him." She looked around.

One of the things about being taller than average was that I got to see more—including the things I was trying to ignore. Like Shayda Hijazi, dancing with Bob, at the edge of the dance floor. I kept catching myself drift towards that spot, and I kept steering away.

Fuck it. I'd had enough.

"Mind if I cut it?" I said to Bob, very much aware of the how quickly the smile on Shayda's face disappeared when she saw me.

Too bad, Shayda. I'm done avoiding you.

"Thank you for saving me a dance, Lizzie," I said.

"Oh no. Thank *you.*" She smiled as we switched partners.

The moment I pulled Shayda into my arms (yes, I had to pull, because she left so much room between us that we could have fit a whole watermelon)—the moment she slipped into the circle of my arms, I fell silent. All the words left me—the clever quips, the sexy teasing, the charming banter. I had nothing. And neither did she. And so we just danced, without agenda, to a slow, smooth ballad. I remember the song, but not the words. Because I couldn't hear, couldn't speak, couldn't breathe for having her near.

She wore a soft coral dress with lace at the hem. It swirled around her knees as we moved across the floor. She kept her eyes fixed on my collar the whole time.

"So," I said after we circled the room. "Here we are, Mrs. Hijazi."

"You remember..." She seemed surprised.

It's strange how someone can walk into into your life, shatter the windows, break down your doors, empty the rooms, scatter your belongings, and then walk away without having the slightest inkling of the storm they'd brought.

Oh. You remember?

"Of course." *Of-fucking-course I remember.*

I thought of the last time I'd seen her, the girl who'd said goodbye to me at the elevator, and I wondered if she still looked at the world with the longing that broke my heart.

"Was it a girl, with sunset red in her hair, like her mother?" I asked.

"Yes," she replied. "But she looks more like her father."

I tried to imagine his face, the man who got to touch her skin, make love to her, fall asleep with her in his arms. Maybe that's what I needed—his face in my head every time I looked at her.

"Are you happy, Shayda?" I asked.

She was supposed to say yes.

And I was supposed to thank her for the dance, escort her back to the table and leave—free, clear and cured. With Helicia in tow.

She said nothing.

And I inhaled her all over again.

"Roses," I said. "I smell roses."

"I'm not wearing any perfume."

"I know."

She had no idea what she smelled like. Maybe it wasn't even real, the way she smelled to me. Maybe it was just me, digging for secret gardens in barren boneyards.

"Your dates are waiting for you," she said.

"Let them wait." *You were supposed to say yes.*

"What?" she asked when she felt my eyes on her.

"That's what I'm trying to figure out," I replied. "What. What is it about you, Shayda Hijazi? There's nothing remarkable about the shape of your eyes or your nose or your face. And yet, when you put it all together, something extra-ordinary happens. Everything clashes. That cool rosebud mouth sets off whatever is percolating in your turkish-coffee eyes. Your eyebrows. Such a proud arch to them. Completely at odds with this demure nose. And when you look away, it's as if some soot is going to fall off your lashes and smudge those chaste cheeks. You're a mass of contradictions, Shayda. All these delicious curves, wrapped around a rod of steel."

"It's called a backbone, Troy. And you don't seem to have one. Or do you just have a thing for married women?"

"I have a thing for women all right." I chuckled. "Delicious creatures, every one of you. Married? Maybe one..."

"Just Jayne then?"

She'd seen it. The kiss Jayne and I had exchanged earlier. Would she be as quick to judge if she knew the truth? I didn't think so, but a gentleman never tells. And I rather enjoyed the fact that it had crawled under her skin, bugging her, laying wormy little eggs that were making her squirm.

"You saw that, did you?" I smiled at her indignation. "Did it offend your sensibilities, Shayda?"

"You think it's funny?" Her eyes flashed the way they had on the stairs that night, the night of the fireworks. "I wonder what Ryan or Bob would say if they knew."

"I wouldn't mention it to anyone if I were you," I warned.

"I'd like to sit down now," she said through clenched teeth.

Fuck her. Fuck her for judging me. For being the one impossible thing in my life.

"You know what I'd like to do?" I yanked her closer. "I'd like to loosen this tight little up-do of yours and let your curls fall free. I'd like to see what you'd be like if you weren't so ruthless with yourself, Shayda."

"Stay away from me, Troy. And stay away from Jayne," she said, tearing away from me and heading for the table.

I followed, a raging tempest brewing inside of me. It pretty much went downhill from there. I downed the dark, stormy clouds she'd stirred up in a succession of cocktail glasses. I stalked her with my eyes, openly, unapologetically. And if that made her uncomfortable and red-faced, *good*. I was back, I was shit-faced and I was done hiding behind some window across the street. I wasn't going to let her hide anymore either, not from me, and not from whatever she had clammed up inside her.

I stood outside, by the stairs to the entrance, and watched her drive away that night. Then I put out my cigarette and took a deep breath. A hint of roses still lingered in the air.

That was the The Summer I Seduced Shayda Hijazi.

6. THREE DAYS

AND NOW HERE SHE WAS.

Four years later.

"Quit fucking with me, Beetroot," I said.

"I'm not. If you still..."

And there it was again, the thing that drove me mad. The fact that she remained clueless.

If you still...

Like it was some personal interest course I'd enrolled in, part time. Landscapes for the Avid Painter, 101.

"I don't know, Shayda. I'd have to check my schedule."

Let her stew. Let her burn. For thinking I would just let her pick up where we'd left off. Under the sheets, me learning the shape of her toes, her trailing her nails down my back.

I walked over to my desk and buzzed Tina.

"I think I'll just get going." Her bottom lip quivered as she headed for the door.

"Tina," I continued. "Clear my schedule for the day."

She whipped around so fast, it made me smile.

I liked her face like that. Toppled over with delight because she couldn't hold it straight.

She gave me an impish grin and held up three fingers.

35

"Hold on," I said.

'Three days?' I mouthed, with my hand over the receiver. "Tina, clear my calendar for the next three days."

"But you have meetings ..." she reminded me.

"I know. Reschedule them."

Nothing was going to come between me and the woman standing before me. That soft-toned watercolor dress she was wearing didn't stand a chance either.

"And Tina?" I continued. "Take the rest of the day off."

I hung up and contemplated Shayda. Maybe if I looked closely enough I might unearth the root of our gnarled connection. We knew better, we knew to stay away, and still we crashed into this glass window, again and again, trying to get to the other side, like a pair of lost, disoriented birds.

"What?" she asked, squirming under my scrutiny.

"Don't ever do that again," I said.

"Do what?"

"Barge into my life and expect me to drop everything for you."

"Don't send anonymous packages to my office then, and pretend like you didn't mean to summon me."

She was right. I told myself I had sent her the umbrella simply to replace the one she'd lost when I'd hauled her over my shoulder, kicking and screaming, out of the storm and into my car last night. That's what I said to myself. Then again, I told myself all kinds of lies when it came to her.

"Touché." I smiled. "You grew a pair. I like that. Now come here so I can kiss you like I've been dying to since the moment you walked in."

She stood over my chair and brushed a lock of hair away from my face. I wanted to feel her fingers on my scalp, tugging my hair, like she did those few seconds before she came. I wanted to slide her dress up and see how much she'd missed me. But I let her sit on my lap, keeping my hands to myself, letting her steer us along.

Her kiss was soft satin—smooth, flowing, gliding—gone before I could grab my fill, like the first notes of a tentative melody. I knew that song well, that buzzing, humming thing she did to my whole body. Desire flared through me as I claimed her lips in a searing kiss. I wanted to violate her with my tongue and my breath and my teeth, to brand her with all of my pent-up agony until she couldn't walk or talk or think straight.

Her arms went around my body, pressing me closer, caressing the length of my back. I felt the old, familiar pleasure, pure and explosive, coursing through my veins, settling in the aching, throbbing heaviness of my cock. Fuck. I hadn't compounded this feeling in my imagination. It *really* was this good with her. And it began from somewhere inside, a place I couldn't see or find or barricade myself against. A place only she knew how to get to.

"You put me through hell, you know," I said.

"We both knew it couldn't go on forever."

"And yet here we are, Shayda. What exactly are we doing?"

"Three days." She tucked her face in my chest. "I haven't thought beyond that."

"Three days, huh?"

She shrieked as I scooped her off her feet.

"We better get going then," I said. "You, my dear, have a lot to make up for." I carried her out of my office.

I had three days to get her to face the truth—that she loved me, that she wouldn't be here if it hadn't left a gaping hole in her heart, that the only reason she wouldn't admit it was because she was scared, because it would destroy everything safe and familiar and predictable in her world.

I didn't care anymore. She would go through hell, but I'd be there to catch her. All I had to do was crush her defenses, lead a seventy-two hour assault on her senses and walk away with her heart in my hand. She would have no choice but to follow.

This was going to be The Summer I Possessed Shayda Hijazi.

7. A CRUEL WORD

THERE ARE THREE THINGS THAT FEEL LIKE SEARING tongues of fire, licking at your soul, each one bringing you closer to the roasting pit of a private hell.

1. Loving someone you can never have.
2. Having someone you love, but never completely.
3. Loving the part of them you can never have, because that too is something you honor, admire, cherish—the part that makes them achingly, exasperatingly *them*.

That pretty much sums up my situation right now. It sucks. It stings. But I know Shayda loves me. Our three days away tell me; the way she melts in my arms tells me; the way she looks at me when she thinks I'm sleeping tells me. And, oh yeah, she put it in writing. It was the cutest thing. I knew she was stepping out of her comfort zone when she traced our initials on a foggy mirror. BB♥SC. Fuck, yes! It was everything she couldn't bring her sweet, stubborn ass to say.

At the time there was no holding back the self-congratulatory high-five I gave myself, but as we drove back, I wanted to take her straight to my place, to protect her from the carnage that lay ahead, even though I knew this was one battle she had to face herself. We both knew what had to be done, and so I watched her get out of my car and drive away, to an unsuspecting suburban house that was never going to be the same again.

There are things in life that break us down, like a demolished pile of rubble, with our insides sticking out, concrete chunks with twisted steel rods that once held us up, exposed and naked for everyone to see. And the whole time we're in pain, we fight it and fight it and fight it, not realizing that we can never build the extraordinary out of mangled foundations. Shayda was about to walk into a wrecking ball, but damn if I was going to sit around twiddling my thumbs.

I wanted to start building—a dream, a future, a place where love could erase guilt, where deceit would be a thing of the past, where Shayda could finally be herself. A place where we could finally be *us*. So I tracked down the owner of the cottage we rented and made her an offer she couldn't refuse. Then I picked up the phone and left Shayda a message.

"Hey. How did it go? Call me back." The cottage was going to be a surprise, but I'd gone thirty long hours without hearing from her.

The next day, I try again. "Beetroot, where are you?"

Three days in. "I'm starting to get worried. Talk to me."

A week later, I snap, my mind spinning all kinds of scenarios about her confrontation with Hafez. She had asked for some time to sort it out, but something feels wrong. Very wrong. She's not at work; she's not returning my calls. There is no way for me to get in touch with her, short of showing up at her door.

And that's exactly what I do. I park a few houses down the street, drumming my fingers on the wheel, trying to keep myself from barging in, no holds barred, and to hell with the consequences.

It's a lazy, summer afternoon. The street looks different from the last time I was here—the rainy night when I dropped Shayda off. Of course, I could have driven past a freaking T-rex, and not have noticed. That's what she does to me.

I note the car in her driveway. It's not hers.

I call her again. No answer.

Fuck it.

I'm about to get out when the front door opens and she steps out.

Relief washes over me. She's all right.

The bunched up knots in my shoulders start to relax.

They tense up again as I watch Hafez follow her, taking her in his arms before Natasha and Zain join them in a family hug, a hug that rips into me like armor-piercing shrapnel. I feel as if a shower of bullets riddled right through me, leaving gaping holes as I watch them through the gleaming windshield of my car—a picture perfect family unit.

This is the family I've been waiting on her to sacrifice. This home, this bond, these kids, that man.

I look away, unable to take any more—the way Zain is clutching Shayda's waist, the way Farah is resting her head on Hafez, the way they've engulfed Shayda like she's the heart of it all.

Damn her! Damn her for making me witness this moment. Damn her for playing house while I've been going bat shit crazy. Damn her for pushing me so close to hating her right now that my jaw hurts from keeping it all in. I thought I knew her, I thought I could see inside of her, but I only saw what I wanted to. *This* is reality. Staring at me in the face. Her and her family.

She has no intentions of leaving Hafez. I'm nothing but a fuck toy, her little shot of excitement on the side. She uses me, gets her fill, and goes back to her life. All these years, the whole fucking push-pull, that's what it's been about. Lies. All lies. And the worst thing is that she doesn't have the guts to own up to it, to tell me to my face that she's been stringing me along. How could I have read her so wrong? How could I have bet my life, my heart, my soul on BB ⊠ SC?

Ragged, jagged pieces of hurt explode inside of me in white hot fury. I get out of the car as Hafez, Natasha and Zain wave goodbye. I don't care if they see me. I don't care if the whole fucking street sees me. The car disappears around the corner and Shayda is back inside by the time I get to the door. I bang on it with clenched fists, and I don't stop until she swings the door open.

I don't know who she's expecting, but it certainly isn't me. Her whole face changes.

"Troy," she says. "You...you shouldn't be here."

She's wearing a wrap-around dress, clutching at the knot that's holding it together at the waist. My body reacts instinctively to her proximity, her voice, her smell, the way her heart is racing so I can pick out the blue-green vein on her neck. I want to take away the power she has over me. I want to pulverize it to the ground until it's nothing but dry, powdered bones.

"No?" I storm past her. "Where should I be, Shayda? Waiting by the phone? Staking out your office? Checking my email? Where the fuck, Shayda?"

I slam my fist into something—a table, the wall? It doesn't register, but I feel a measure of satisfaction when she jumps. I want to stop wanting her, needing her, and I'm ready to destroy anything in my way, ready to hurt anyone, including her.

"I changed my mind." Her voice trembles, and she can't bring herself to meet my eyes.

If I hadn't witnessed what I saw outside, I might have been taken back, incredulous, taken in by her flawless act. But now...now I'm just fucking furious.

"You changed your mind. Just like that? And when were you were planning to tell me exactly? When, Shayda?"

"I made a mistake," she says. "I got caught up in the moment. We were alone, we were away. It was...it was all an illusion."

"An illusion?" I want to shake her, but I bring her up against me so hard, I feel the air expel from her lungs. "Is this an illusion?"

I bear down savagely on her lips. I want her to feel it, feel *me*.

Illusions don't leave your lips swollen and red and raw.

At the first taste of her, I feel my control snapping. "And this?" My fingers dig into her thighs. I know they'll leave bruises. But it's not enough. I want her hurting on the *inside*. Like I am.

"What about this, Shayda?" I nudge her panties aside and enter her roughly with my fingers. "Tell me, Shayda. Tell me this is all in my head."

I take a few steps forward so I have her up against the door. Then I deepen my strokes. Her reaction is instantaneous, a rush of sweetness that sets me throbbing.

"Tell me this is nothing," I challenge. "This is you, Shayda." I push my glistening finger past her lips and into her mouth. "Your taste, your smell, your skin, your touch. Tell me you're not real, Shayda. Tell me!"

My breath comes in quick, hollow breaths. I feel myself getting sucked into her dark, almond eyes. How can they stare back at me with such longing and pain, so innocent and pure, as if...as if this is the truth and everything else is a lie?

Her phone rings, but I keep her pinned against the door.

I'm not done until I fathom the depths of her soul, until I've unlocked every facet of this exasperating, heartbreaking woman in my arms. Why would she freeze me out when she's eating me up with her eyes, like she hasn't seen the sun in days?

The answering machine picks up. "Hi, Shayda. It's Lisa from Dr. Mason's office..."

Shayda pushes me off and runs to the phone.

"Your mastectomy has been scheduled for September 12th..." The lady at the other end continues.

I stop listening and rewind the message in my head.

Your mastectomy has been scheduled...

Your mastectomy...

Mastectomy...

A jarring crash interrupts the deathly echoes bouncing around in my head.

The answering machine lies broken on the floor.

Shayda swings around, her eyes burning with something so intense, I feel scorched in its wake.

"Are you happy now?" She shoves me back towards the door.

"You still want to hang around?" *Pain.*

"Watch them cut my breasts off?" *Excruciating pain.*

"Maybe you'd like to see my bald head? Huh?" *No.*

"Hold a bucket while I puke my guts out?" *No no no. Just no.*

With each word, I die a little.

With each word, I let her push me towards the exit.

"Get out, Troy!" She holds the door open. "I can't stand your butterfly dreams or your perfect love or your perfect world. You hear me? I can't stand it!"

I'd asked for this. I'd wanted to know why she'd locked me out. And now that she was telling me, I didn't want it.

Take it back.

Tell me it's not true.

Tell me I'm nothing but your fuck toy, your little shot of excitement on the side.

God. I'll take anything.

Anything.

Just. Not this.

All those ugly thoughts I'd had about her, and all the while my Beetroot was doing what she did best. Putting everyone else first. She'd been shielding me from the truth. And that hug...the hug I'd witnessed outside had been a family coming together in crisis.

I stand by the door, staring at her—hurting, guilty, broken, ashamed. I don't think I could have loved her more. How is that possible? When you think you've reached the very edge of love, that you can't possibly go any further, and then the circle gets stretched a little bigger. And the pain with it.

"Go!" She gives me one final push and turns away.

I stand frozen, trying to find the words that will stop the bleeding. For me. For her.

Her shoulders slump when I shut the door; she sinks to the floor and doubles over.

She thinks I've left.

As if a few cruel words can push me away.

As if one cruel *word* can keep us apart.

She didn't have to say it.

Cancer.

She had mentioned losing her aunt to it, mentioned taking her mother for mammograms. But it's the kind of thing that stays on the periphery, like a wall you walk by every day. You never really notice it until it comes down.

I feel like I've been running, running, running—two paces from the finish line, and that's when it collapses, another obstacle in a never ending race. I want to howl at the unfairness of it, but I have to be strong. I've seen Shayda like this once before—when she thought she had lost Zain.

If I had to pick a definitive moment when I knew I loved Shayda, it was then—when I witnessed her agony. I knew she was blaming herself for Zain's accident. I knew I would have dredged up the entire lake with my bare hands if that's what it took to get him back. I knew the girls, the parties, the booze, were all distractions, a safeguard to protect myself, because I didn't want to give all of myself when I could only have pieces of her. But that day...that day, I would have given up everything for a bit of diamond dust. When the ambulance door shut, and I saw the look on her face, I knew I had lost her.

I wasn't going to let her do that again. I wasn't going to let her push me away.

"Don't," I say, when her soundless sobs become too much to bear.

She turns to me, eyes filled with shock and shame when she realizes I'm still there. If she could have hidden somewhere, away from my gaze, she would have, but she is so spent, so exhausted, that she just lays there like a rolled up, wilted rose petal.

I stretch out on the floor beside her. "I'm not going anywhere. I told you. Whatever happens, we face it together. I know you're doing this to protect me, but I'm not going to let you shut me out. Not again, Shayda."

When I take her in my arms, she lets out a deep breath, like she's been relieved of some heavy burden.

Yes. We'll share it, this weight, this uncertainty. Whatever it brings.

I try to control the spasm in my throat as I stroke her hair.

You can't have her, I say to the powers that be. *Fuck you.*

No, fuck you, Troy.

I'd forgotten about the sparring match that fate and I had started way back, on the night of the fireworks. The dirty bastard was still in the ring, taking jabs at me.

I might be down, but I'm not out, I reply. *And I'm ready to go all the way to gates of Hades for her.*

8. BARBED WIRE

I PUSH MY PLATE AWAY AND MAKE A POINT OF NOT LOOKING at my watch. My first day in Hong Kong has been productive. Long, but productive.

"Finished, Mr. Heathgate?" Raymond Zhang smiles at me.

It's no secret that he's out to woo me—not personally, but he most definitely wants my business—enough to drop everything and hold court while I'm in town. It would be a lucrative partnership for both of us. I need his contacts; he needs my resources.

"Thank you for dinner." I reply.

"My pleasure." He finishes the last of his dessert, a mango pudding with translucent black squares of grass jelly. "What time would you like me to pick you up in the morning?"

"Eight would be perfect."

"Done." He gets up and gives me a slight bow. "Call me if you decide to sleep in. You never know what distractions our beautiful city might have in store for you." He gestures to the panoramic views of Victoria Harbour from our table.

Another time I might have ventured into the cosmopolitan metropolis, with its sparkling sky scrapers, where opera singers rubbed elbows with fortune tellers, and street vendors sold souvenirs and snacks in ordered chaos. But tonight I find myself yearning for a quiet moment to call home.

And by home, I mean Shayda. The last time I'd seen her, she'd been watching soft, feathery snowflakes come down from the window. She didn't have her wig on, and the way the light fell on her bare head made me catch my breath. My Beetroot. She'd been so strong through all of it.

"There's something I've been meaning to tell you," she'd said to me after her surgery. We were on the phone—me, in a conference room in Monterrey, and her still recovering in the hospital.

I think it was easier for her to do it that way, rather than in person, where she'd have to look me in the eye. Maybe she thought she'd see something there that she didn't want to. Horror? Pity? Or maybe the only way she could get it off her chest was in a drug-induced haze.

She didn't stop once she started. She kept going as if a pressure valve had been released and all the words were clamoring to get out in a long stream of sentences: the truth about a Nowruz that changed everything, the secrets that haunted her marriage, the filth that was Pasha Moradi.

She hung up before I could say anything. I stared at the receiver for a long time, letting the missing pieces of the puzzle fall into place. I thought I'd uncovered everything there was to know about the attempted rape she'd suffered, but it had roots I could not have fathomed. I felt for Hafez, but my protective instinct kicked into overdrive. I wanted to swaddle Shayda up and carry her away from all the things that had weighed her down.

On the way to my hotel that evening, I asked the driver to stop at the local market. We'd passed the colorful stalls many times, but that day something caught my eye. It swayed in the wind, among a sea of browns, blacks, purples and blues—a single red shawl, tugging at the clothes line, straining to be free. The old lady who sold it to me pointed out a few flaws in the weave, urging me towards the other pieces, but I thought it simply added to its charm. It was only when I gave it to Shayda that I realized how fitting it was, how some things become more beautiful with imperfections, like patina on bronze.

Tomorrow I might find something just as fitting for her, from this corner of the world, but tonight I'm exhausted.

"Goodnight, Zhang," I say.

He nods in acknowledgment as we shake hands.

I take the opulent gold and glass elevator to my room, a few floors down from the rooftop restaurant where we dined. My tie is half off by the time I enter, but something makes me stop and inspect the dimly lit suite. There is a slightly sweet smell, like ylang ylang and musk, that wasn't there before.

"Good evening, Mr. Heathgate."

I follow the soft, breathy sound of a woman's voice and make out a figure lounging on the chaise by the window. The moon highlights her shiny black hair. Her milky skin is barely covered by a silk robe.

What the fuck?

"My name is Mei Li." She takes her time getting up so I can appreciate her petite, curvy frame.

Her dark eyes are demure, but beguiling. When she steps into the shaft of light from the bathroom door, some of her quiet composure deserts her. Momentarily. Then she lowers her gaze with a gleeful smile.

"Mr. Zhang did not tell me you're so...striking. I'm here to make sure you're comfortable."

"Comfortable?" A part of me is amused, a part is slightly alarmed at the very male reaction I'm having to her—her scent, the exotic inflections in her speech, her barely suppressed sexuality. I wouldn't call it comfortable.

The thought of Zhang sending me a high paid escort for the night is secondary. I've seen enough of the world, dealt with enough businessmen to understand that hospitality means different things in different countries.

"May I pour you a drink?" Mei Li drops her robe, as if nudity were a pre-requisite to mixing a manhattan.

It's been a while since I've seen another woman naked.

She's nothing like Shayda. Perhaps that's why I can stare at her pert, full breasts with detachment, mentally comparing them to the harsh, dual slashes on Beetroot's chest. It feels strange—my cock is twitching, but with an empty, hollow desire, like a jaguar with sharp, ready teeth, regarding willing prey with the nonchalance that comes from a sated stomach.

Shayda fills me, she settles in that place of hunger. There is no space, no *need* for anyone else. Do I miss the softness of her breasts? Hell, yes. Just as I miss teasing her nipples and feeling them grow hard in my mouth. But there is a satisfaction that goes beyond arms and legs and skin and lips, beyond touch and breath, to that intangible realm beyond the primal, where bodies disappear into souls, and the music is so sweet, you don't even notice.

So I let Mei Li pour me a drink. She brings it to me and then sits on the bed.

I have no problems with a naked woman playing bartender in my room. Hell, I can even appreciate it. But there's only one woman who belongs in my bed.

I place my glass on the nightstand and hold out Mei Li's discarded robe. "Thank you, but I won't be needing any more drinks tonight."

She takes the robe, but refrains from covering herself. Instead, she reclines on the luxurious jacquard bedding, giving me an eyeful of prime, alabaster perfection. "You don't like what you see?"

"On the contrary. You're a beautiful woman."

Mei Li angles her head and regards me with curiosity. "You prefer men?"

"No, my dear." I laugh. "I prefer women. Very much."

"Women?" She keeps her eyes on me. "That can be arranged. You want more than one?"

"I just want one."

"I don't understand."

"I want one woman, Mei Li. And she's not here with me."

"Oh. You have someone back home?" She crawls on all fours towards me, like a cat begging to be stroked. "I don't see a ring." She stops and licks my finger, the one she expects a wedding band on.

"I don't need a ring."

"That's not fair to other women, is it? Nothing that says 'Private Property.'" She deliberately checks out the outline of my package through my pants, aligning her mouth with my cock.

It's pretty obvious I'm not immune to her charms.

"I'm very discrete," she says. "And I can make you very, very happy." The 'happy' part escapes like a sigh through her lips. Her fingers tip-toe over my chest to undo my collar.

A deep chuckle escapes me. This is a first—having to defend my honor before an overly eager courtesan.

"How much is Zhang paying you?" I pry her deft little fingers away from my half open shirt.

"Forget about Zhang. This one's on the house."

"How much?" I repeat, more forcefully this time.

She sits back on her heels and quotes a number.

My eyebrows must have shot up because she gives me a suggestive glance.

"I am highly trained in the art of pleasure," she says.

"I have no doubt," I reply. "It still sounds like an exorbitant amount."

"It's not just for tonight. He hired me for the duration of your stay."

I take a sip of my drink and grin. "Well, that's about as ironic as a screen door on a submarine."

"Excuse me?"

"Never mind. It's time you get dressed."

She pouts, but slips into the robe before heading into the bathroom.

"Mr. Zhang won't be too happy about this," she says as she zips up her skirt.

"Zhang doesn't need to know. I'll be sure to thank him for setting up an interesting interlude. Have you been compensated for your services?"

"He gave me half. He was going to settle the rest when you leave." She comes out of the bathroom, taller in her stilettos, with clothes that speak of expensive logos.

I open the in-room safe and hand her an envelope. "I trust this will make up for an early goodbye."

Her eyes widen as she looks inside. "That's a lot of money to stay away from someone."

"There *is* one thing I'd like before you go," I reply.

"So you're not made of stone, after all." She puts the envelope in her jewel encrusted clutch and snaps it shut with a triumphant click. "What would you like me to do?"

I pick up my glass and mull over it. "Many years ago, a woman asked me to make her a promise, to let her know when I got serious about someone."

Mei Li looks at me uncomprehendingly, but my thoughts are elsewhere.

I remember that afternoon, playing with Shayda's hair as we sat on the floor of my office, thinking we'd be safe as long as we kept a certain distance—no promises, no expectations. I didn't want to give her an excuse to leave, but I wasn't about to paint the reality of our situation with rosy hogwash. At some point we'd realize we were on a burning train. She'd bail, or I would, or perhaps we'd both wake up one morning, with blisters on our skin from where we'd touched, and decide to walk away. Yet somehow, all these years later, we were still chugging along. And we hadn't turned to ashes.

It was time I kept that unmade promise, time I let her know just how serious I was. About her.

"Mei Li," I say, rubbing the jet lag out of my eyes as the idea began to take form. "Do you know of a tattoo parlor that would be open at this time?"

It had taken a practiced seductress to make me realize that I didn't need to take home a fitting gift for Shayda. I needed to *make* her a fitting tribute—one that *did* say 'Private Property'. And what better way to do the job than with barbed wire?

9. ENOUGH

I BUTTON UP MY SHIRT, MY SKIN STILL TINGLING FROM THE little bites Shayda left across the tattoo emblazoned on my chest. My hand touches the empty spot where my rosary used to rest and I break into another foolish grin.

She said yes.

It wasn't so much that she said yes, because regardless of whether she admitted it or not, she'd said yes to me a long time ago. This went further than that simple world, miles beyond the Shayda I'd run into that summer morning, so many years ago. This was Shayda breaking out of her cocoon, daring to reach for her own happiness, allowing herself, allowing *us* to set things right.

My grin grows wider as I spot her bright red lip print on my thigh.

Beetroot Butterfly Unleashed.

Zhang comes online before I have the chance to slip into my pants, so I sit through the video chat in my shirt and boxers, before his company's very solemn board of directors. We nail down some specifics before I give Zhang the go-ahead for our collaboration. My phone rings as I'm getting ready to leave the suite.

"What would you like for dinner?" my mothers asks.

"You're on vacation, Ma. Save the cooking for when you get back. Besides, I thought you and Dad were meeting Bob and Lizzie tonight."

"They canceled. You know the nice couple we met at New Year's? The wife gave that eloquent speech on breast cancer? I forget her name. The one who works with Bob? Oh. You bought your loft through her."

"Shayda."

"Yes. That's her. Well, her husband had a terrible accident this afternoon. Bob just called from the hospital."

Silence.

"Troy?"

"I'm here. I just..." I clear my throat, trying to shake off the sense of dread that's shackled me. "I have to go."

"But what about din...?"

I hang up and grab my coat.

***

IT'S A TWENTY MINUTE DRIVE TO THE HOSPITAL. EVERY stop light, every sluggish, dawdling car, every second that ticks by is like a slice of hell.

Please. Don't let this be because of a confrontation about the affair.

What do you care, Troy? You did this. You pushed her. You had to have all of her.

Yes. YES! I want her. All of her. But not at Hafez's expense.

No? I must have missed that clause. Here. Let me grab my reading glasses, Fate taunts. *No. Nope. Nothing here. You really have to learn to be more specific when you ask for things. There are consequences to every action, and it's time for me to collect.*

I pull into an empty parking spot and call Bob for the details. Probably not the most discrete move on my part, but I don't give a rat's ass. Lizzie picks up.

She seems surprised, but gives me Hafez's room number. "Bob's still there. Tell him I'm bringing a casserole. I doubt anyone's eaten anything..."

For the second time that day, I hang up mid-conversation.

Wheelchairs and attendants and groups of families are crowding the elevator. I take the stairs, two at a time, to Hafez's floor. The cold, sterile hallway flashes by in a blur as I try to locate the room I'm looking for. The door is closed. I peer through the small square window and see Shayda, sitting with her back to me. Natasha is leaning against the wall, arms crossed, and Zain is standing next to her, kicking the floor with short, half-hearted jabs. They're all watching the man on the bed, tethered to beeping machines with wires and tubes.

I stand outside, separated by a double glazed panel of glass, my little hole into their world, torn between opening the door and stepping inside, or backing off and respecting their time together as a family.

I dial Shayda's number.

She jumps, as if from a trance, and looks at the screen. *Pick up. Pick up, Beetroot.*

But she lets it go to voicemail and goes back to watching Hafez.

I try again.

Come on, baby. Turn around.

On the third ring, she looks at the phone again.

I know she's blaming herself, blaming *us*, for whatever happened to put Hafez on that hospital bed. Still, I can't help but flinch when she swings her arm back and throws the phone, throws the screen that's flashing my name, at the wall. Natasha and Zain stiffen as it clutters to the floor.

"Who is it?" asks Zain, his eyes wide with disbelief at Shayda's outburst.

"No-one," she replies.

I feel the blood curdle in my veins.

It's a day of simple words, loaded with meaning.

The *no-one* she said *yes* to a few hours ago.

The *no-one* she agreed to spend the rest of her life with.

The *no-one* whose rosary is dangling from her wrist.

I will always be the *no-one*. Because everyone who counts in her world is on the other side of the door.

I will always be on the perimeter of her life, always the outsider, always looking in.

The realization punches me so hard, I reel from the sharp, twisting pain in my gut.

All those years of waiting and wanting are torn from me, like chapters of my life being ripped apart. And that's when it hits me. Just how weary and exhausted I am, how tired of holding on and hoping. I'm tired of love, tired of loving. I'm worn down to my bones, achy and ragged from this soul-marathon. My heart hurts, my head hurts, the air in my lungs hurts.

I need to get off this ride, once and for all, to stop this tightness in my throat when I see her hair cascading down the back of her chair, this mad devotion to a woman holding vigil over another man, this tingling chorus my fingers are singing to feel her skin, her mouth, the softness of her cheek.

Had enough, Troy?

Enough, Fate. I step away from the door, like a soldier conceding defeat, bloodied and battered, ready to be dragged away like a bag of bones.

10. TAIL OF THE DRAGON

IN THE LAST FEW MONTHS, I'VE CONQUERED FOURTEEN OF the most grueling motorcycle routes in the world, riding through harrowing turns of tarmac, across vast swathes of empty desert, and glaciers lined with ice and gravel, at times being baked alive in my leathers, at times facing stinging hail and blinding snow. The brunt of the elements is exactly what I need to numb the pain. I welcome the cramped knuckles, and knees that sigh with relief at the end of the day. Sometimes I ride past the pain, testing my boundaries through the night, as far and as fast as I can, hoping to leave everything behind.

***

RUNNING HAD NOT BEEN ENOUGH. FOR DAYS AFTER HAFEZ'S accident, I pounded the pavement until every tendon, every sinew screamed in protest. When I got home one night, sweaty and gasping for breath, my parents were packed up and ready to leave.

"I baked you some treats," my mother said, as she kissed me goodbye.

"Take care, son." My father thumped me on the back.

They looked resigned. I suspected they had skipped their annual winter getaway in the hopes of fixing me up with Gabriella. My only regret was that I'd been so out of it that their presence had barely registered. It had been the same at work. I was there, but not really. I got through the day like a clockwork zombie. Alive outside, dead inside.

And I hated it. I hated not feeling that zest for life, that burning hunger to taste and see and savor things with my whole being.

I missed being me.

I placed my water bottle on the kitchen counter and caught site of the cookies my mother had baked. She'd stored them in the same glass jar that Shayda used for brownies. It was wide mouthed with a brushed aluminum lid. Clear and simple and solid. Unlike anything Shayda and I had ever shared. We were shifting sands and murky waters, unsettled secrets that never found ground.

She hadn't called to prove me wrong. Not a note, not a message. All her words and promises felt dead and hollow.

I looked around the loft and wanted to empty the space of her—her smell, the sheets she slept on, the desk she wrote on. I didn't want to see long, curly strands of her hair on the bathroom floor, feel the emptiness of crawling into bed without her. My hands tightened around the cookie jar. I wanted to smash it into the ground, watch it break into a million irreconcilable pieces. I couldn't be here, stay here, eat and breathe and sleep here. I needed to exorcise her, put everything I felt for her to rest.

I put the jar back down and made a call.

"Sam," I said, when my assistant picked up the phone. "I'm taking a leave of absence..."

***

AND SO HERE I WAS, MONTHS LATER, WITH A COOKIE JAR full of rubble strapped to my bike. It was mostly pebbles from the beach, mixed with remnants of the pile left behind by the renovation crew when I'd stopped by our cottage to get my bike.

Correction. *My* cottage. There was no *our* anymore. There was only me, and this final 120-mile loop of the Cherohala Skyway and the Deal's Gap, a stretch of US Route 129 that ran through the Great Smoky Mountains. Dubbed the "Tail of the Dragon" because it contained over three hundred challenging curves, this is route number fifteen, the last on my list.

Although spectacular views await at every turn, the twists and switchbacks require my undivided attention, something I find both liberating and exhilarating. I stop at the Tree of Shame, a makeshift shrine to those bitten by the Dragon. Draped on its branches are mangled motorcycle parts—tires and helmets and headlights—bits and pieces of mishaps, some minor, some fatal. In the middle of winter, it looks abandoned and forlorn, with broken aspirations hanging like ghosts from its frame.

I have my lunch there, feeling a certain kinship with the sad, comical looking tree. It's the one thing left standing—alive in spite of all the dead dreams.

I'm done carrying the weight of dead dreams. My face feels leathery from the sun and rain and snow. I've slept under open skies and seen stars where there were none before. I've survived the toughest tracks, endured the harshest trials. I've taken the time, I've licked my wounds. I salute the tree and put my helmet back on. It's time for me to see this through.

At Cheoah Dam, I pull out to take in the view, where Harrison Ford made his death-defying leap in the movie, 'The Fugitive'. Here was another man, devoted to the woman he loved, running, running, running. It seems fitting to find myself here, at the end of my journey. There's just one thing left to do.

I unstrap the cookie jar from my bike, take out one of the pebbles and close my eyes.

A golden street. A girl with sunset red in her hair. A boy on his morning run. Papers flying everywhere.

"Don't move. There's a butterfly. On your shoulder."

My fingers are rough and cold against the smoothness of the pebble. I hold it for a second, weighing that moment, that first meeting, before I toss it over the edge and watch it disappear, grey on grey, into the frothy waters below.

One memory down. A jar full left to go.

I pick up the next pebble. One by one, I say goodbye.

Goodbye, roses.

Goodbye, fireworks and mad duck and girl clinging to me in a lily white dress.

Goodbye, stolen dance and stolen kiss and almond eyes and golden thighs.

Goodbye, drowning boy and rainy night and red umbrella.

Goodbye, afternoon tea and bundt cake face.

Goodbye, scarred chest and warm brownies.

Goodbye, 'x'. Goodbye, 'o'.

I reach for the last pebble and take a deep breath.

Goodbye, Beetroot Butterfly.

I bounce the pebble off the side of the dam. It skips once, twice, before being swallowed up by the thundery, white water.

I continue staring into the churning foam, even as the wind picks up and my ears go numb.

I've turned my heart inside out and emptied all the chambers. My pilgrimage is complete.

I take a long pull on my cigarette before stubbing it out under my boots.

It's time to head back and reclaim my life.

11. GOODBYE

I DRAIN THE LAST OF MY DRINK AND LOOK AROUND THE
empty loft, thinking of the day I'd seen it the first time.
Here, by the door to the pool, I'd caught Shayda's reflection.
Different from the day I caught her watching Bob's family,
and yet still the same. Somewhere down the road that sad,
broken look had been replaced. I wondered if she still smiled
with her eyes, the way she did when she saw me walk in
the door, sometimes with flour in her hair, sometimes
looking up from her writing. It wasn't my business anymore.
She wasn't my business anymore—what expressions flitted
across her face, what thoughts filled her head. I was done
with being the runner up—always silver, never gold. I was
done with stalling and excuses and non-decisions.

I pick up two boxes and take the elevator down. I've
been at it for a few days—sorting, packing, arranging for
the move. The Toronto branch of my operations has been
well managed in my absence, and I'm ready for a fresh start.
I feel an old, familiar restlessness seep into my bones, the
kind that tells me it's time to go back and embrace the bright
lights and buzzing energy that is New York.

I slide the boxes into the trunk and glance at my watch. Just enough time to catch up on some correspondence at the airport lounge. One more trip upstairs and I'll be on my way.

I let myself back into the loft, but stop in my tracks, unprepared for the sight of *her,* standing in the hallway, clutching at the wall with that same damn, broken look that always gets me. It lifts the moment she sees me.

"I thought I'd missed you. I thought you'd gone," she says, taking a step towards me.

No. I've exorcised you. Dragged your demon entrails on the back of my bike until they turned black and lifeless.

I don't want you here. I don't want you near.

I veer for the last box and start making my way back out.

"Troy! Troy, wait!" She grabs my arm and spins me around.

I burn at the touch of her. If I let her, she'll incinerate me, pour my ashes in an urn and scatter them where I'll never be found.

All these months, not a single call, not a glance back, and *now* she shows up? At her fucking convenience? To yank me back like a dog on a chain?

I turn around and let her see. The big, fucking 'Private Property' vibe radiating from my whole body.

No trespassing, bitch. It might have been yours once, but I'm taking it back. Stay *the hell away.*

"Troy, I'm sorry. Hafez was in an accident. I—"

"I know. There's always something, Shayda. You promised me, you bound yourself to me. And all that changed the moment you stepped out of that room. I get that you wanted to be there for him, but you turned me off— like a fucking switch. Just like that. I'm done, Shayda."

I haven't said her name in months. Not out loud.

It comes out like a fibrous slice of flesh that I've chewed on and chewed on, and spit out.

She takes a step back—maybe because she can't stomach the way it sounds, maybe from the force field of sheer hostility around me.

That's right.

"You don't get to yank me around anymore," I say. "Not after everything I've laid bare for you. I don't want you or your dead promises or your mind-fucking, poison kisses."

"I can explain—"

"Get out of my way, Shayda. I have a plane to catch."

Enough justifications. Declarations. Fabrications.

"Troy, I—"

I unleash the full force of my fury in that one look. All the dead hopes, the corpses of dream bodies, the cadaverous chambers of my heart file through in one final funeral procession of *us*.

"Goodbye, Shayda Hijazi." I get in the elevator and press the button down.

She doesn't say it back. She just keeps staring at me until the doors close, and the last I see of her is a narrow slit of her rosebud mouth.

12. CHAI

I TAKE GREAT PRIDE IN MY STAFF'S COMPETENCY, BUT TODAY
Celine's robotic efficiency is grating on my nerves.

She gives me the entire run down of my next meeting—
numbers, clients, market share, assets, challenges—before
dropping the bomb on her way out.

"There's someone here to see you. No appointment."

Her perfect hand-writing, professional and impersonal,
leaps at me from the note pad.

How could she write it like that? Shayda.

No capitals, or bold, or underline, or exclamations.

No warning bells or fat, red pen or devil horns doodled
with a sharpie.

Just Shayda. Plain and nondescript, like any other office
memo.

No. Not just Shayda.

Shayda Kazemi.

I sit back and stare at it.

There's only one reason she'd use that name. She's
divorced.

And here.

Waiting outside.

You know the rules. No appointment, no meeting, I open my mouth to say.

"Send her in," I find myself saying.

I'm not one to run and hide. If she's here to see me, let's be done with it. Married or divorced, she can't touch me anymore. That ship has sailed. You only get so many chances. But I *am* curious about why she's here, in my fort, in my world.

She enters hesitantly, her demeanor clashing loudly with her tough leather jacket and ruby red lips—the shade she wears only for me.

I tighten my grip on Celine's obscenely normal note.

"What can I do for you? Shayda...Kazemi." I force my eyes back on the paper.

Her maiden name feels foreign. She's always been married, always someone else's woman.

"I was hoping we could talk." Her eyes dart across the length of the conference table, but I like it there between us, reminding me of the leap she could never make.

"So talk." I indicate the seat at the other end of the table.

"I'd rather stand."

"Suit yourself."

What do I care that she's lost so much weight, that her cheeks have receded, making her eyes look like that of a fawn, that her hair has grown back in little flicks around her face?

"You didn't tell me you bought the cottage," she says.

Is that why she's here? She figured it out and concluded I was in the throes of some misguided nostalgia for what used to be?

"I wasn't aware I needed to keep you apprised of my investments," I reply.

"I rented it for the week."

"Yes, my property manager forwarded the info."

It had come as a surprise, seeing Shayda's name on the list, but the initial shock was quickly followed by anger. No doubt she was planning to spend time with Hafez there. A cozy reunion of sorts.

I had signed off on it, the final nail in the coffin. Strangers rented the cottage; strangers went in and out of the space that had once been ours. And when all was said and done, she qualified as one. All I knew of her life now were the bits and pieces Bob or Jayne brought up in passing. They'd mentioned that Hafez had recovered, and was back home. No permanent damage. I had felt relief, tempered with the bitterness of feeling like everything was back in its place, as if I had never happened.

"Amy?" Shayda's voice cut through my thoughts. "Amy is your property manager?"

"Shayda." I tap my pen on the table, trying to figure out what could possibly have gone wrong. Why was she using her maiden name when I'd freed her from making the decision she'd always been loath to, taken away the choice she could never make? "Why are you here?"

"Because I love you," she says. "Because I miss you. Because I was empty before you and I'm empty after you. Because the only time I've felt truly alive is the time I've spent with you."

It's nothing I don't know. I know what we had, what she meant to me, what I meant to her.

But I know now that love is not enough. It was never enough. Love is what blew us apart—too much of it, too raw, too painful. It smashed us into so many pieces, I can still hear the rattle of it in my bones.

"I do recall asking you to marry me," I say. "But then you had a change of heart."

You always had a change of heart.

"It's always been you, Troy. Always."

69

Always is such a bullshit word, a lie, a farce, a road that promises to go on forever. But roads, like life, branch off, and merge and meander. And they both always, always end.

"Let me get this straight," I say, to this magnificent woman I fought so hard for, this magnificent woman I fought equally hard to be free of. "You think you can march in here with your hot lips, in that sexy outfit, and expect me to just roll over? Because you're bored and lonely now? Because you've decided you'd like to have me around, after all?"

I expect her to wither, to give up, to leave with her tail between her legs, because that's what she does when the going gets tough. She gives up on me.

But she surprises me.

"Don't do this, Troy," she says. "Not when we're finally here, at this perfect intersection; when we're finally free to be together."

"What makes you think I'm still free?"

"I don't care!" She slams a clenched fist on the table.

That gets my attention—Shayda making a fucking fist, like she's ready to punch whoever is keeping me from her.

"Make yourself free." Her eyes blaze. "You're mine, Troy. And I'm not giving up without a fight. I've learned that I matter; what I want matters. So here I am. I get that you're hurting—I get that you want me to hurt too. And I'm sorry, Troy. I'm sorry for shutting you out. Time and time again. But I know you. Every cell, every edge, every fibre of your being. You miss me just as much as I miss you."

I'd forgotten how spectacular she is like this, when all the fire and pent-up emotions rise to the surface, and the blood boils like lava in her veins.

This is Shayda, fighting for me. Fighting like hell. Unexpected, uninvited. A valiant battle in the board room. For *us*, the *us* she always put last.

And I have to admit, I'm really digging it.

"Do you know what this is?" She slides a photo towards me.

I look at the image and try to place it. "It's a photo of me, from years ago. I'm rollerskating with my neighbour, Carol, on the boardwalk by my parents' place."

"It was tucked away behind your parents' photo. The one from your loft. You remember, you had it on the shelf in your living room?"

"You came all the way here to show me this?"

"Look again, Troy."

I look where she's tapping, but all I see is the pale band around her finger, where her ring used to be. Then I see a face peeking at me from the faded print behind it.

I pick up the photo and take a closer look. "Is that...is that you?"

A younger Shayda, but with the same golden skin, her knees drawn to her chest, watching us with the wind blowing in her hair.

"It was you, Troy." Her voice cracks with emotion. "The day I went looking for a sign. I saw *you*. I wanted to be the girl holding your hand, I wanted us to be that couple. We were like two stars converging around the same axis, but with paths that missed each other by a fraction of infinity. And so we passed each other by. Don't let that happen again, Troy."

What day? What sign?

All I know is that I stopped believing in stars and paths and destiny, the day I lost the battle with Fate, outside that hospital room, as I watched Shayda and the kids huddle around Hafez.

She'd come, she'd made her case and she'd fought like hell. I had to give her kudos for that. This was a different Shayda, a Shayda I would have given anything to see before—

71

stronger, truer and impossibly sexier to me. But now I'm the one who can't make that leap. I can't afford to track back and let myself believe all over again. It would be like opening the sutures to an old wound, to make vulnerable what's finally healing over.

I push the photo away. I've said goodbye to a lot of exes, but the words have never tasted so caustic, so corrosive that my tongue wants to curl up and die. "I told you, Shayda. I'm not free."

How can I be? With my heart caught in your heels? It hurts when you walk towards me, It hurts when you walk away.

She doesn't flinch or back down. She's like a giant, refusing to be slain, bent on pulling out the part of me I tried to drown in that dam, the part that's breaking through the surface and threatening to come alive again.

"Kiss me, Troy." She leans in, her lips just inches from mine. "If there really is no room for me in your heart, I'll know. I'll walk out of here and you'll never see me again."

Once upon a time, I'd walked into her office and done the same.

Kiss me, Shayda. It can't possibly be as good as it is in my head. I'll walk out of here and we'll both be free.

And look at where that had led us. Bloodied hearts. Wasted years. Pain. Separation. Anguish.

I start to rise, closing the gap.

My nostrils flare with the smell of roses.

I can feel her breath on my lips, so erotic that I have to grip the edge of the table to keep from grabbing her.

One whisper soft touch and I'd be sucked right back in again.

"I don't have to prove anything to you," I grind out and head for the door.

She sways like the earth has just been pulled from under her feet. I wonder if I staggered the same, outside Hafez's hospital room when she threw the phone. There's a moment of excruciating silence as she makes an effort to collect herself. Then she squares her shoulders and turns around, gripping the rosary around her wrist.

It will bring you light in the dark.

I hope it does. I hope it does, Shayda, because I'm running on empty and I have nothing else to give you.

She walks past me and the air fills with her. I want to suck it in and never breath out again, but I hold the door open and watch her march into the lobby. My throat is on fire from all the words burning to come out, all the words I'm choking back to keep from stopping her.

I chug down a tall glass of water to drown it out, to give myself something to focus on.

Un-fucking-believeable, Fate whispers in my ear. *I offer her to you on a silver platter and you turn her down.*

I know better than to tangle with you.

Oh come now. I'm not all bad. Not my fault if you two missed each other on that boardwalk.

I pick up the photo Shayda left and trace her face.

What if I had turned around? What if she'd walked past me, brushed against me? Would I have felt her, smelled her, sensed her?

There is a tiny glint of silver around my neck, where the cross on my grandma's rosary had caught the light that day. The whole family had been at the beach. That was the day Uncle Jim had come to pick up Chai, my grandmother's dog, named after her favorite tea, a golden assam blend—the same shade as Chai's fur.

After Grandma passed away, we'd taken Chai in, but with me in college and my parents away so often, Uncle Jim had offered to look after him. Chai was just like my grandmother, doting and devoted—slobberingly affectionate with us and equally snarly with strangers. Taking Chai out for a walk was always a a challenge. The boardwalk was rarely deserted and Chai growled at anyone who got too close. But that day, he sat on top of a sandy hill, ignoring everyone, sniffing the air, as if he knew he was leaving. And he would not budge. My parents said goodbye, my cousins took off, Carol took a few stabs at rollerskating on her own and returned, Uncle Jim tried to woo him with treats, but Chai did not move. When we finally managed to lure him into the Uncle Jim's car, he bounded from the other side as soon as his leash was off.

"Chai!" We chased after him.

He ran down the hill, straight for a lone figure sitting by the boardwalk. In spite of his surly temper, he'd never attacked anyone, but he'd been acting strange all day. Uncle Jim let out a cry as Chai fell upon the stranger, but we watched in amazement as he proceeded to slobber all over her.

"Does he know that girl?" asked Uncle Jim.

"I don't think so." Between Chai's wagging tail and the girl's squeal of delight, all I could make out was a blur of long, curly hair. Then Chai turned around and dashed back to us.

I look at the photo again and feel like I've just been kicked in the ass.

Well, fuck me sideways.

My grandmother's golden retriever is long gone now, but in my hand is a picture of the girl he'd displayed uncharacteristic affection for, the girl who, as we speak, is walking out of my life with my grandmother's rosary.

Still don't believe in stars and paths and destiny, Troy?

Shut the fuck up, Fate. I have a woman to reclaim.

Maybe we can shake hands when you get back?

Maybe. But you're still a sonofabitch.

I rush out of the boardroom and see her making a bee-line for the exit, head held high, shoulders squared like she's afraid she might run into something and shatter. For one satisfying, sadistic moment, I hold back, savoring the fact that I know something she doesn't—that in a few minutes the dimple on her left cheek is going to make an appearance, that she might have come here alone, but she sure as hell isn't walking out on her own.

"Wait." My voice projects across the lobby. "I believe you have something of mine."

She stalls, looking like she might bolt, because she can't take more pain, more humiliation.

Then she turns around and looks at me. "Sorry?"

I know she heard me, but she's just buying time, because when our eyes meet like that, it takes a minute for the heart to catch up.

"You have something that belongs to me," I say.

I'm talking about her, my Beetroot Butterfly, but she thinks this is about my rosary. She starts walking towards me with a pinched expression, holding her hand out, offering me back the last, remaining piece of me she thought she was getting away with.

I almost smile. I am *so* going to hell for enjoying this, but damn, I love watching the woman I've loved so long fight to hold on to every bit of me, for as long as she can.

She stops a few feet away, the tremor in her wrist the only sign of her inner turmoil.

The chaos of buzzing phones and office conversations, the hum of the lights above us, the notes in my head about the next meeting, everything fades away. I feel a stillness settle around me. It seeps through my skin and pours into me like warm, golden syrup, filling my bones with a sweetness I never thought I'd know again. I feel like the first time I saw Shayda, on the sidewalk, before I knew she belonged to someone else. Except this time, she's mine. And I want nothing more than to kiss the silver scar on her lip where she'd split open, to stave that flow of pain and seal it with a promise—that I was never, *ever* going to let her go again.

I yank her into my arms and take full advantage of her silent 'oh' to plunder her mouth. I exhume all the things I buried on my bike—the honeyed taste of her, that first brush of her tongue when we kiss, the soft, little sound she makes when my teeth graze her lips. I claim the arms she winds around my neck, the delicious curve of her back, the tips of her toes that are raising her up to meet my kiss. I claim her because now, here, finally, I *can*.

The brutal ferocity of my kiss eases when I feel her go slack in my arms, like I've sucked out every last bit of doubt and tension, answered all the questions, melted all of her bones and left her breathless and stupid-faced and dazed.

"Don't you ever, *ever*, walk away with what's mine, Beetroot," I say, when we come up for air.

"I thought you'd put up more of a fight, Scary Cherry." She puts on a brave front, even as her face turns the brightest shade of red, because everyone around has dropped what they were doing and they're cheering us on.

No doubt this piece of prime office gossip is going to make the rounds for weeks.

"I lose it. Every time you barge into my office." I growl in her ear. "Every fucking time,"

"Heyyy—"

"I know, I know. Stop swearing. Stop smoking. Stop drinking..."

"Which leaves just one other option," she replies, her face bursting into the widest smile ever.

And there it is. The damn dimple I've been waiting to score.

"Let's get out of here, Beetroot." I expect her to protest when I pick her up, but she snuggles in.

Let them see. Let the whole world see.

"Sir, your meeting..." Celine calls after us.

"Tell them something came up," I reply, loving the sound of Shayda's giggle. "Tell them Troy Heathgate has left the building."

I get in the elevator with my woman and throw my jacket over the camera.

EPILOGUE

....

I LOVE THE WAY THE MORNING SUN PICKS UP THE RED glints in Shayda's hair. It's grown out this past year, so I can take a strand and wind it full around my finger. She wore it down yesterday, an uncommon bride, in a Beatles t-shirt that echoed mine. No heels for her either. We stood bare feet on the circle of pebbles on the beach, marked by the 'x' where we'd watched our first sunrise.

****

IT HAD BEEN WARM FOR EARLY SUMMER, BUT THE BREEZE from the lake left a trail of goosebumps on Shayda's skin. Or maybe it was from the culmination of the long journey that had brought us here, before our friends and family—an acceptance, an affirmation, that prickled her flesh with the kind of happiness she never thought we would find.

News of our involvement had not been well received. My parents were skeptical, her mother enraged. Jayne had sulked. Bob and Lizzie tried to disguise their shock. The kids turned distant and rebuffed our attempts to get them engaged.

The world had put on us trial, found us guilty and locked us out. Shayda swung between bouts of exasperation and despair, at times convinced we deserved it, at times infuriated by the endless battle for acceptance. We weathered the storm together, having come much too far to turn back, and slowly the tides started turning—first Zain, then Natasha. Eventually, Jayne invited us over for dinner. Bob and Lizzie came by. My parents asked for Shayda when they called; her brother and father stopped by when they were in town. Shayda's mother continued to voice her disapproval, but realized that her only other option was to cut her daughter out of her life. And she needed Shayda a lot more than Shayda needed her. Whatever the reason, over the course of the year, they all came around, slowly, one stepping stone at a time. And their presence at our wedding made Shayda latch on to me with such joy, that I smiled through the entire ceremony like a forty year old virgin about to lose it.

We cut a giant bundt cake in the gazebo that Jayne had adorned with garlands of soft, pink roses.

"Told you he'd be the last man standing," said Ryan to his sister.

"Oh, he fell a *long* time ago," replied Jayne. But she coughed up the $10 they'd bet years ago.

My parents didn't know what to make of the barbs Shayda's parents exchanged, but Bob and Lizzie buffered the situation. Of course, no-one could do much about the awkwardness that lingered between Hafez and me. It had been a year since his accident, and although our paths had crossed many times because of the kids, the wedding was different. I knew how difficult it must have been for him to attend, and I respected him all the more for it. When Natasha and Nathan disappeared, we tracked them down separately and found ourselves face to face by the shed near the lake. The kids were sitting on a log, drinking beer. Hafez and I were both silently relieved that's all they were up to, but of course we took away the beer, ignored the eye-rolling and sent them back to join the party. Then we stood there, the father and the step-father, feeling like we should high-five for a job well handled. There were things I wanted to say, things he wanted to say, but we mumbled and fumbled our way through two bottles of confiscated beer instead. The rest would come in time, I hoped.

At night, Shayda's brother, Hossein, and I set up a bonfire on the beach and we all sat around, while Zain played his guitar. Shayda's mother was still wearing her hat, a big, fluffy concoction with blue-black plumes.

"Just so we're clear, if a spark drifts off and one of her feathers catches fire, do you want me to go with this or that?" I asked Shayda, pointing first to the water, and then the bottle of vodka in Ryan's lap.

"You're terrible," she said, smiling sleepily as she snuggled into me. "And keep your hands to yourself. She has x-ray vision."

"How much longer before I can respectfully carry you off to bed?" I continued stroking her thigh under the blanket.

"We're not leaving until everyone's ready to head back in."

"Fuck that." I tossed the blanket and pulled Shayda up.

I couldn't see her face as I carried her off, but I grinned, knowing she was cringing because I had I reminded everyone, including her, that it was our wedding night and I wasn't ready to share her with anyone.

***

And now sitting here with her, with *my wife*, the morning after, I grin some more. "So you think your mum and dad did it last night?'

"Troy!"

"I don't see your dad getting up this early in the morning. I think he was sneaking back into his room."

"I don't want to talk about it."

"Why, Beetroot, I do believe you're blushing, red as the sun rising before us. Just when I think I've done and said all the things that will make you squirm, I find something new."

She shakes her head and pulls her red shawl closer around her.

"What?" I ask.

"I've married a man whose mission in life is to torment me."

"Consider it payback for all those years you tormented me."

"You ain't seen nothing yet. Just wait till I have my new boobs, mister."

"About that. I'm feeling very left out of the whole decision."

"Because I kicked you out during the consult?" she asks.

"Yes! All those boobs and you made me wait on the other side."

"You were like a kid in a candy story. Did you have to feel them *all* up? There was no way I was going to let you talk me into those double d's."

"But they were so jigglicious. I'm not sure if you've really thought this through."

"Troy?"

"Yes?"

"Sun." She points to the horizon as golden rays break over the lake.

I nuzzle in and claim her lips. "Good morning, Mrs. Heathgate."

She doesn't stop smiling when I pull away. "I think I've found my second most favorite sound," she says.

"The first being...?"

"The way you say my name."

"Shayda?"

"You don't hear it, do you?"

"Hear what?"

She laughs like she's holding a big, bubbly secret. "I love you, Scary Cherry."

I trace the barbed wire ring tattooed around her finger. "I have something for you, Beetroot. I'll be right back."

When I return, I place a cookie jar in her lap.

"What's this?" she asks.

"A wedding gift."

"An empty jar?"

"It may be empty now, but the point is to fill it up." I pick up a pebble from the center of the 'x', the one on which the painted lines intersect, and put it in the jar.

"Soooo we're going to fill it with pebbles from the beach?"

"Not pebbles. Memories. One at a time. This one's for today, for the crossroad where I finally get to call you my wife."

"Nice." She peers into the jar. "Hey, isn't this my brownie jar?"

"It is."

"Regifter," she accuses.

"Recycler," I counter. "Reduce, reuse, recycle. You're the one who's always going on about that."

She makes a face and walks around the shore until she finds two giant pebbles. "My turn."

"Those aren't going to fit, Beetroot."

"They're not for the jar."

She pitches one into the water with a quick snap of her wrist. Instead of skipping across the surface, it sinks with a loud plop.

She holds out the other one, waiting for me to take it.

"Too big. Too heavy. You need a lesson in picking the right stones," I say.

"They're not skipping stones."

"Then?" I give it my best shot, but it nosedives straight into the water.

"Those were your double d's, Troy. Say goodbye because they're never making it into the jar."

"What?" I yank my shirt off, my pants are half-way down my knees when she pulls me back.

"There's no saving them tatas." She's laughing so hard, I take a mental snapshot.

"Maybe not, but there are some pebbles at the bottom of a dam that I might have to retrieve."

"Huh?"

"Tail of the Dragon. You remember when I took off?"

"You mean when you went sulking off on your bike?"

"I prefer to think of it as slaying some mighty dragons, but that's a discussion for another day. For now, I have one more gift for you."

Her eyes widen when I hand her an elegantly wrapped box with a bright, red ribbon.

She holds it up to her ear and gives it a shake. "It's not a butterfly."

"No." I laugh.

"Roller skates!" she exclaims when she opens the box.

"That's right. And we're going to build a private little boardwalk right here, so you can use them."

"And you're going to teach me?"

"You seem to thrive on private lessons, Beetroot." I watch the flush steal across her face. "That's twice I've made you blush before breakfast, Mrs. Heathgate."

"Like I said, I've married a man whose mission in life is to torment me." She threads her fingers through mine and kisses the tip of my nose.

We listen to the rhythmic splash of the waves as the sun climbs higher.

"We should go get breakfast started," she says after a while.

"Remind me how we ended up hosting both sides of the family on our honeymoon."

"Mum?" We hear Zain calling from the cottage.

"Down here." I reply.

He joins us, still sleepy and mussed up. Natasha follows, trailing a blanket, and plops herself between Shayda and me.

We sit in silence, enjoying the moment, before Zain's tummy lets out a ferocious growl.

"Come on." He pulls us away.

We follow the kids back to the cottage, but before we enter, Shayda turns around and looks back at the lake. I follow her gaze, past the gazebo, down the stone tiles, to the reflections of dancing sunlight on the lake.

I'll always remember it this way—The Summer I Married Shayda Heathgate.

"Here we are," I say, pulling her back and holding on a little longer.

"Here we fucking are," she replies.

There's a moment of stunned silence before I turn to her.

"Don't look now, Scary Cherry," she says, "but you have bundt cake all over your face."

THE END

ABOUT THE AUTHOR

LEYLAH ATTAR IS *A NEW YORK TIMES, USA Today and Wall Street Journal* best selling author, who writes stories about love—shaken, stirred and served with a twist. Sometimes she disappears into the black hole of the internet, but can usually be enticed out with chocolate.

Connect with her at
WWW.LEYLAHATTAR.COM

OTHER TITLES BY LEYLAH ATTAR:
53 LETTERS SHORT STORY
THE PAPER SWAN

www.ingramcontent.com/pod-product-compliance
Lightning Source LLC
Chambersburg PA
CBHW020546130626
46552CB00007B/2777